Space Bugs and Selfies!

A story about being yourself, space bugs and farting.

Lex Genn
Illustrated by Simon Collins

Illustrated by Simon Collins

First published in the United Kingdom in 2018 by
The Choir Press

ISBN 978-1-911589-48-8

For Tillybug
and all the little people
who should never be told who to be.

Lily likes stories and running downhill
and naming frogs Susan and Laura and Bill.

And flying a dragon who helps fight the baddie,
then farting quite loudly and blaming her Daddy.

Her jeans are bright green, her gold socks are fun and her favourite top has a big fox's bum.

With big curly hair all over the place,
she's always got snot or mud on her face.

Then some girls at a party said,
"You could be pretty,
you just need to be
a little less... gritty."

They all said, "With effort you could look sweet,
you can't be a princess with hair that's not neat."

"And then you can hang with all the cool girls
and chat about nails and big eyelash curls."

"We love high-heels, big hair and make up, and all swap our selfies each day when we wake up!"

So, Lily went home
to scrub herself off
and put her green jeans
in the box, for the loft.

She said goodbye to her lovely gold socks
and off came the top with bum of the fox.

She brushed and tidied her curly black hair,
then found a pink dress down the back of a chair.

She secretly borrowed some make up from mum
and felt really grown up when it was all done.

Her pink dress was perfect
and made her look sweet,
her hair was all straight
and exceptionally neat.

When they saw Lily, the girls were so pleased.
She looked just like them, from hair to cold knees.

They pointed at boys and they giggled their chats,
about clothes and shoes, and who looks this or that.

But soon, Lily found, it was yawningly boring,
to talk about shopping and nails all morning.

When she told them her dragon was fun but quite lazy,
they looked at her like she'd gone totally crazy.

None of them cared about what she loved,
like flying through space on an alien bug...

...or smelling a new smell, or surfing with cats, or watching the clouds, or wearing eight hats,

or playing piano, or learning karate,
or practising blaming your Dad when you're farty.

So she washed off her make-up,
then dumped the pink dress,
and happily pulled her
green jeans up her legs.

She grinned as she put on her shiny gold socks,
and on went the top with the bum of the fox.

out!

She thought of those girls
and of losing her place,

then smiled at the thought
of fresh mud on her face.

FAT!

She ran from the bathroom
and felt really glad,
then let out a farrrt
and screamed,
"IT WAS DAD!!!!"

The stinky but happy end

About this book

I wrote this book after talking to a friend about something that happened to their six-year-old daughter. She'd come home from school, mortified because some other girls had said her thighs were fat. It's irrelevant but this little girl is slim, athletic and far from anyone's idea of fat. But that didn't matter. She was hurt and damaged by the experience.

I was bullied at school myself, so know just how much it hurts and the long-term effects. I wanted to tell all the little people it didn't matter how they looked, who they were or what other people said; especially my three-year-old daughter. But all the books I found about body positivity and self-confidence were for older children. So, I wrote one. And I gave the story to parents and kids; and then to a fabulous illustrator called Simon. And here we are.

About me

I've been surrounded by strong women for my whole life; my mother, my sister, my aunts, my nanna, and now my indefatigable wife and wonderful daughter. I'm a feminist and see feminism as good for everyone, whoever they are, however they identify.

Resources

If you want to find more great stuff for kids and more useful ideas, have a look at these sites:

- mightygirl.com – a huge selection of books with positive messaging
- girlrising.com – a global campaign for girls' education and empowerment
- guiltyfeminist.com – hilarious, thought-provoking and supportive podcast about trying to be a feminist, despite the programming and judgements of the patriarchy
- wowfest.uk – Women of the World Festival
- therepresentationproject.org – inspires individuals and communities to challenge and overcome limiting stereotypes, so everyone can fulfil their potential
- amysmartgirls.com – emphasizing intelligence and imagination over fitting in

Lightning Source UK Ltd.
Milton Keynes UK
UKHW05f2253130518
322458UK00001B/2/P